WILD DESIRE

WILD HEART MOUNTAIN: WILD RIDERS MC
BOOK FOURTEEN

SADIE KING

WILD RIDERS MC

AN INTRODUCTION

Welcome to Wild Heart Mountain home of the Wild Riders MC.

If you love damaged heroes and curvy girl romance, then you'll love the Wild Riders MC.

This group of ex-military bikers fall hard and fall fast when they encounter the curvy women who heal their hearts.

Expect forbidden love, age gap, forced proximity, fake relationships, single dads, single moms and off-limits love with protective heroes who will do anything for the women they love.

Spend some time with Wild Heart Mountain's Wild Riders MC, the MC that's all heart.

Let me introduce you to the members…

Ex-military buddies **Raiden, Quentin and Travis** formed the Wild Riders MC when they got out of the military and wanted to create a place for veterans who love to ride.

They set up their headquarters in a compound on the side of Wild Heart Mountain.

Travis, whose road name is Hops, runs the Wild Taste Bar and Restaurant, and secretly crushes on his best friend's sister.

Quentin, also known as Barrels, runs the award-winning Wild Taste Brewery located out the back of the restaurant. He was a First Class Sargent in the army and you wouldn't want to cross him. Especially where his little sister is concerned…

Colter, or Vintage, is a motorbike mechanic and runs the bike shop. He collects old bikes and loves all things vintage, especially the bubbly Danni and her 1950s curves.

Calvin, also known as Badge, is the local Sheriff and his uptight views are shaped by loss.

Joseph, or Lone Star, is a recluse whose military experiences have given him a distaste for humanity.

Grant goes by Snips. He's the local barber and recently

discovered he has a child. He's learning to navigate life as a single dad.

Arlo earns the road name Prince because of his charming and personable nature. He loves getting under the skin of Maggie, the shy pastry chef.

Davis begins the series as a prospect. Younger than most of the other men, he came out of the military with diminished hearing. His hearing aids make him shy with women and he keeps himself hidden away.

Specs would rather read a book than talk to anyone.

Bit Rate is a grumpy single dad widower in need of a nanny.

Judge is a military lawyer and always does the right thing, until he meets the curvy woman who makes him question his world view.

Luke becomes a prospect after Raiden finds him drinking himself to oblivion in a strip joint. A wheelchair user since he lost both his legs in Afghanistan, Luke finds new purpose with the MC, but can he find love?

Marcus goes by Wood because his family owns the local sawmill and it's his medium of choice. He channels his PTSD into his art, creating sculptures that attract the attention of an arts journalist from the city.

On the other side of Wild Heart Mountain is a town called Hope, with the Emerald Heart Resort nestled in the nearby hills. During the summer, it's a popular destination for tourists and in winter, they come for the ski season. Perfect for a snowed in romance…

Stay awhile in Wild Heart Mountain and explore the other series set here.

Wild Heart Mountain: Military Heroes
Wild Heart Mountain: Mountain Heroes
Temptation
A Runaway Bride for Christmas
A Secret Baby for Christmas

WILD DESIRE

WILD RIDERS MC

She needs a date. I need her...

Cassie's trying to get the attention of her parents, and she thinks dating an older bearded biker will make them take notice.

Problem is, this hairy biker wants the real deal.

I agree to a fake date, but only until I can convince Cassie she belongs with me.

Now she has her parents' attention, and they don't approve of me running around with their little girl.

Too bad I'm not letting her go.

Wild Desire is a fake relationship, age gap, steamy romance between an ex-military biker and the curvy girl he refuses to give up.

1

CASSIE

"*H*appy Birthday to me..." The song echoes through the dark and empty house, and when I stop singing, only silence greets me.

I blow out the candle on the double chocolate cupcake from the birthday batch I made myself this morning. As I bite into the cupcake, the hard icing cracks under my teeth, and for one glorious moment I forget I'm alone on my birthday again.

I flick the lights on and take the last of the cupcake and a mug of hot chocolate to the living room. My favorite armchair has a coffee table next to it, and I place the cupcake and hot chocolate next to the paperback I'm currently reading. Then I climb into the armchair and pull the fluffy pink blanket around me, getting cozy in my nest.

I check my phone, but there's still no message from my parents. They both left for the office early this morning. I heard them in the kitchen, and I came down wondering if Mom was making me a special birthday breakfast.

I was just in time to see her grab her keys and head out the door. Dad at least said hello before he grabbed his coffee thermos and followed Mom. They work at the same office, for a wine importing business that's made them rich, yet they take separate cars to work.

I was left in the oversized kitchen, the empty counter stretching before me like my empty day.

I pick up my book from the coffee table and open it to where I left off. A gold edged piece of thick paper falls onto my lap, and I pick up the invitation I'm using as a bookmark.

When the mail arrived at noon and there was a letter addressed to me in the handwriting of my mother's assistant, I stupidly thought it was a birthday card. But no, it was an invitation to a corporate event next Friday night, a party they're hosting at a local winery for their business associates.

Yup, my parents sent their own daughter, who lives in the same house as them, an invitation in the mail.

That about sums up the relationship I have with my parents.

I put the invite on the coffee table next to my cupcake and hot chocolate and turn my attention to my book. It's just getting good. The tension between the alien overlord and the curvy girl he's holding prisoner is ratcheting up a notch, and if they don't at least kiss soon, I'll explode with anticipation.

His tentacle tightens around my neck, and he drags me toward him.

"You're mine, Bailey, in this universe and the next."

My eyes widen as another tentacle snakes between my legs...

My phone vibrates, rattling the glass coffee table. I think about ignoring it so I can find out where the alien overlord is about to put his third tentacle, but when I glance at the screen, it's Isabella.

My best friend is not the kind of woman who is easily ignored. If I don't answer her call, she's likely to show up on the doorstep with her huge hairy biker husband.

"Happy Birthday, bella." She draws out the words with a hint of the Italian accent inherited from her father.

I try not to smile too much at her words. Isabella texted me this morning to say happy birthday, but this is the first time anyone's uttered those words to me today. Not that I should care. Twenty-three isn't a special birthday. I should be over wanting cake and presents and nice things like, say, my parents remembering it's my birthday.

"Sorry I didn't call earlier; Marco wouldn't settle, and the little patatina growing inside me is restless today." I imagine her rubbing her round belly.

The latest pregnancy has been hard on Isabella and her overprotective husband is demanding she rest, which is something Isabella has never been good at.

"It's fine," I say. "I've had a great day."

Isabella grunts, and I can almost hear her frowning down the phone. "Define great."

I glance down at my tea-stained pajamas that I didn't bother changing out of this morning. "I've spent the day reading and baking cupcakes. I'm onto my third book."

"Oh honey, I'm so sorry. I should have come around. But Raiden dragged me to the hospital again."

Concern flares for my friend. "Why, what's wrong?"

"Nothing's wrong, which is what the doctor told Raiden. It's just bad morning sickness. They kept me in all morning and did a scan. I'm fine, the baby's fine. Raiden..." She gives a throaty chuckle. "My husband is not fine. He's anxious and stressed and pacing the place like a wounded lion."

Raiden is the President of the Wild Riders Motorcycle Club. The burly veteran is used to solving problems, and a difficult pregnancy is not something he can fix.

"But you're sure you're okay?"

"Positive, bella. I've rested all morning, and now I'm restless. Which is perfect because we're going out to celebrate your birthday."

She says it so fast it takes me a moment to realize what she's said. "Wait, what?"

Isabella chuckles. "You didn't think I was going to let you get through your birthday without a celebration, did you?"

Only Isabella knows without asking that my parents forgot my birthday. It was the same every year when we were away at private school. Her father came to visit her every year on her birthday to take her out. Mine never even called. Isabella took it on herself every year to make sure we celebrated. The tradition stuck.

"You don't have to do this. You've got your own family to think of now. And I'm fine staying in and reading, honest."

Isabella continues as if I've said nothing. "Get yourself dressed in something nice. I hope you don't mind that I'm not up for going anywhere far, so we're having something at the clubhouse."

The clubhouse is the Wild Riders MC headquarters. Isabella spends half her life there, and I've gotten to know some of the other bikers and their wives over the three years since she married Raiden.

They're not as intimidating as they first seem. All the bikers are veterans, and they're a legit club. They own a brewery behind the headquarters with award-winning beer, and they run a restaurant with amazing views over the valley. They're a nice bunch of people.

Still, I'm comfy in my PJs with a hot chocolate and my book.

"I'm okay, really. I don't want to intrude on the club. I'm okay here."

"Oh no you don't," Isabella says sternly. "Get out of your pajamas and put on something nice. We're celebrating your birthday."

I don't remember telling Isabella I was in my pajamas, which goes to show how well she knows me.

She was always like this, cajoling me into going out when all I wanted to do was stay in and read. Trouble is that half the time she's right. If it wasn't for Isabella, I would never leave the house.

"But…" I glance at A *Curvy Nanny for the Alien Overlord.* I really would like to know what happens when he gets all three of his tentacles in action and whether he'll give up his kingdom for a quiet life on earth with the earthling he loves.

"I think I'm going to sit this one out."

"Not an option," Isabella says. "Maggie's made a birthday cake."

Maggie's the pastry chef at the club restaurant, and her baked goods are to die for. "What flavor?" I ask, despite myself.

"Double chocolate."

It's my favorite. Maybe it wouldn't be so bad going out, and yet my book and hot chocolate in my favorite armchair also sounds good.

"Get yourself ready. One of the guys is coming to pick you up."

By one of the guys, she means one of the Wild Riders MC. "On a motorbike?"

"Of course."

"But…" I pull the blanket around me, trying to hunker down in my cocoon. "Don't send anyone. I'm not sure I want to come out."

"Too late. Specs already left."

My mouth goes dry at the mention of Specs. He's the club's accountant with a wayward beard and sparkling eyes behind his glasses, which got him the road name

Specs, and he always carries an e-reader tucked into his jacket pocket.

"You sent Specs?"

"He volunteered."

Panic floods me. I'm not ready to see the hairy biker with the kind eyes. "Tell him not to come. I'll get a car."

There isn't a ride share company this far up the mountain, but my parents have people who work for them that I can call. I'd rather have a driver come and get me than ride on the back of a motorbike with Specs.

"Too late. He already left, remember?" Isabella sounds pleased with herself, and I wonder if she's noticed how nervous I get whenever Specs is around.

I hear the roar of a motorbike outside. I jump off the couch and check the security cameras in the kitchen. At the gates is a man dressed in biking leather and strad-dling a Harley Davidson.

"He's here."

If Isabella hears the panic in my voice, she ignores it. "Good. We'll see you soon."

But I don't hear Isabella's last words.

Of all the bikers she had to send Specs. Then I remember that Isabella told me he volunteered, and my belly does a flip. Whenever I'm around Specs, my shyness goes to 100%. The man makes me forget my own name.

The gate buzzes and my finger hovers over the open button, wondering if I should let him in. But it would be rude to turn him away.

I push the button to open the gate and watch as he glides across the courtyard and to the front door.

7

2

PAUL

*T*he iron gate slides open silently, revealing the mansion on the other side.

"Well damn," I mutter to myself as my gaze sweeps over the whitewashed stone buildings that surround the cobblestone courtyard.

Vines grow up the sides of the walls that stretch out on either side of the gate, disappearing into the dusk and the gloom of dark gardens beyond.

I roll my bike over the threshold and cruise across the courtyard. The damn thing's so big it takes a good half minute to get to the front entrance. There's a water feature in the middle with a fish standing on its tail spouting water into a round pool.

The entire place has a European feel to it, like I've been transported into a casa in Spain. Not that I've even been to Spain, but I've read books set there.

A second-story balcony provides an overhang where

the front door is, and I park my bike next to it and kill the engine.

I slide my helmet off and run my hands over my hair before pressing the doorbell.

I'm expecting a butler or someone in a smart uniform to answer the door, so I'm surprised when it opens and Cassie peers out.

My breath catches at the sight of her wide eyes and round face peering at me.

"Hi…Happy Birthday." My voice comes out in a nervous stutter, and I clear my throat. "Isabella sent me to pick you up."

She presses her lips together, still hiding behind the door.

"Are you ready?"

The door opens further, and I get a glimpse of what she's wearing. Pale pink pajamas with roses on them. The fabric clings to her hips, showing off her curvy figure. The tight pajama top pulls across her chest, and I'm pretty sure she isn't wearing a bra.

My mouth goes dry, and I pull my gaze away from her chest.

"I need to get changed." Her voice is soft, like a caress across my heart. "Come in."

Cassie opens the door, and I follow her into the entry-way. It's as vast as the courtyard and just as sparse. The walls are wider than my entire cabin, and the only furniture is a thin sideboard, with a blue vase and no flowers.

"I brought you this." I pull a package out of my pocket

and hand it to her. It's plain brown paper wrapped in string, but her eyes light up at the rectangle shape. "For your birthday."

She takes the package. "Thank you. You didn't need to get me anything."

"I know."

She opens the package, and I watch her eyes as she turns the book over in her hand. The cover is worn at the edges, and some pages are folded over.

She frowns, and then her eyes go wide as she reads the title. "*The Art of War*. This is the book you were telling me about." She looks up, and the delight in her eyes lets me know I've done the right thing.

We talk about books, Cassie and I. It's a safe topic, and last time I saw her, three months and two days ago at Luke and Isla's wedding, we got into a lengthy discussion about my favorite classic. She's never read *The Art of War,* so when I learned it was her birthday, I knew the perfect gift.

"This copy was in Iraq with me. There's probably sand in the pages."

She holds the book to her chest. "Thank you."

"I know it's not what you usually read…"

"I read all sorts," Cassie interrupts. "My favorite is, um, women's fiction. But I'll read anything, especially off a recommendation."

I smile at her comment. I know for a fact that Cassie loves reading romance, but if she wants to call it women's fiction, then I won't contradict her.

She leans against the wall and thumbs through the

book. Her earlier self-consciousness about being in her pajamas is forgotten as she stares at the words on the page.

She curls a strand of hair around her finger as she reads.

I could stand here and watch Cassie read all day, especially my favorite book, but Maggie has baked a cake and Isabella's gotten everyone together. Isla decorated the place, and there are balloons and drinks and good food waiting.

I clear my throat and Cassie looks up, blinking.

"Sorry, it's...the opening."

"I know, right?"

She's as into the book as I hoped she would be, and a surge of warmth rushes through me.

"You sure you don't want to stay here with me and read instead of going out?" She's smiling as she says it, and I can't tell if she's serious.

I'd like nothing better than to spend a night quietly reading with Cassie, but Isabella will kick my ass if I don't bring Cassie back. And yeah, I'm kind of a little scared of the Prez's old lady.

"That's temping. But it's your birthday, and there will be cake."

She gives me a smile that pierces straight to my heart. "I need to get ready. Give me ten minutes."

I follow her through to the living room, which is an open area with large gray couches. One armchair in the corner has a blanket bundled on top of it and a coffee table next to it. Cassie scoops a book from it as she goes past before I catch the title. I get a flash of the cover, which features a muscular male torso that's tinted green. The man has horns and what looks likes tentacles coming out of his body. I pretend not to notice the 'women's fiction' as she tucks it under her arm.

"Feel free to watch the TV while you wait."

I pull my Kindle out of my pocket and hold it up. "I'm good."

She nods, and I settle on the couch with my book.

3

CASSIE

*T*he Harley throbs between my thighs as I cling on to Specs. The pavement rushes past beneath my feet, and the wind whips against my cheeks. It's my first time on the back of a bike and my fingers dig into Specs's waist as I press myself against him, certain he must hear the hammering of my heart through his jacket.

It's exhilarating, and when we arrive at the clubhouse, I think about telling Specs to keep riding. I wonder what it would be like to ride with him up the mountain, to find a secluded spot, just the two of us.

I shake the thought out of my head. There is no way a man like Specs would be interested in me. He's at least a decade older than me, and he's a veteran. He's had a life. What would he want with a spoiled twenty-three-year-old?

We pull up outside the clubhouse, and Specs parks at

the end of a line of Harleys. Reluctantly, I slide off the bike and hand him the helmet. Our fingers brush, and electricity jumps between us. Specs's eyes widen, and he looks away. He hangs up the helmets and I retrieve my purse from the saddle bag, wondering if I imagined the heat between us.

My heels clack across the pavement as we head into the clubhouse. I changed into tight black slacks and my only boots with a low heel.

As I walk into the bar area of the clubhouse, I'm greeted by loud cheers. Most of the club is here with their wives and kids. A Happy Birthday banner hangs above the bar, and there are streamers and balloons.

Isabella comes forward to hug me with a huge grin on her face. "Happy birthday!"

"Thank you," I squeak.

My parents may have forgotten I was born today, but Isabella never forgets. I'm filled with warmth for my friend. Since she married Raiden, the MC has become her second family, and they seem to have adopted me as well.

Sydney hands me a cocktail. She's Bit Rate's sister and has recently returned to the mountain. "Happy birthday, hon." Her silver bracelets jangle in my ears as she hugs me, and I get a waft of her strong perfume.

I sip the cocktail. I'm not a big drinker, but it is my birthday. More people step up to say, "Happy Birthday," and I'm caught saying hello and catching up with the eclectic group of people who have become my friends. When I look around, Specs has faded into the crowd.

The lights go dim, and everyone starts singing "Happy Birthday." Maggie comes out with a chocolate cake with blazing candles and sets it on the bar.

"Make a wish, bella," says Isabella.

I close my eyes and think about the one thing I want. Next birthday, I don't want to spend the entire day alone. I open my eyes and blow out the candles. As I do, my eyes meet Specs's over the bar. He smiles and nods, and warmth fills me from the inside out.

"Birthday shots," says Isabella.

My face falls and I tense.

"Only joking," she cackles. "I'm pregnant, and you don't do shots. But here, have birthday cake instead."

Maggie cuts me a large slice, and I retreat to a table as everyone crowds the bar to grab their piece. As they do, I wonder if it's an opportunity to sneak away. Not that I don't like a party—I appreciate everyone being here—but after an hour of talking to people, my energy is waning.

One of the rooms at the clubhouse has been made into a nursery for the kids, and it's often quiet. I take my cake and head in there.

Marco is asleep in the crib, and one of the older kids is playing with Legos.

I take the armchair in the corner, and with my cake in hand, I pull out my book; *A Curvy Nanny for the Alien Overlord.* I set the bookmark down on the armrest and settle in.

I'm not sure how much time has passed, but I'm startled by someone coming into the room. I look up to see Specs.

"Thought I might find you in here."

He takes the armchair next to me, and as he sits down, his thigh brushes against mine. Sparks of heat shoot up my leg. I squeeze my thighs together and focus my attention on the man.

Specs picks up the invite I've been using as a bookmark and frowns as he reads it.

"I didn't think you liked parties."

"I don't." I frown, wondering if I sound ungrateful. "Except for birthday parties that have been thrown for me. They're great."

Specs chuckles. "You don't have to explain it to me. I'm the same. I like seeing my people—but an hour or two will do."

He studies the invite, and his finger traces the gold edging. "This looks fancy."

"My parents sent it to me. Can you believe that? In the actual mail."

Specs raises his eyebrows. "Don't you live with your parents?"

"Yeah." I sigh.

"Why didn't they just give it to you?"

"I don't know. It came in the mail today. I thought it was a birthday card.

"Ouch," He mutters.

"It's an annual party they throw for all their suppliers and distributors. It will be nothing like this casual get together at the clubhouse. No kids allowed, no cake, not shots.

"Everyone will look the same; the men in suits, the women in tasteful two-pieces, with designer jewelry and high heels. There will be champagne and waitstaff in matching uniforms and hors d'oeuvres so tiny you have to eat fifty of them to feel full."

Specs looks at me. "Then why go?"

It's a good question. I'm twenty-three years old, a grown adult. I don't have to do anything for my parents anymore. Yet... there's something in me that's still hopeful. That maybe, if I turn up to their party and speak politely to their guests, they'll notice me.

But there's also the chance they won't.

There's a good chance I'll turn up and speak to some of the guests. They'll tell me how much I've grown into a beautiful woman. One of Dad's friends will try to get hands-y. I'll have to put my back against the wall, and after an hour, I'll slip away and find somewhere quiet to read.

My parents won't notice I'm there, and they won't notice I've gone.

Anger flares through me suddenly, making me tremble. They should notice me. They should notice their daughter.

"Are you cold?" Specs shrugs off his leather jacket. He hands it to me and drapes it around my shoulders.

I don't want to tell him it's anger making me tremble. I wish there was something I could do to make my parents notice me.

"Thank you." I pull it around me and breathe in the

scent of him, leather and motorbike grease and old books.

"It looks good on you."

He gives me a shy smile and curls the corner of his beard. There will be no one at my parents' party with a beard. Perhaps a few older men with mustaches, not even ironic ones.

A thought bolts through me so suddenly I sit upright, and my book tumbles off my lap. I go to snatch it, but Specs gets there first. He glances at the cover and hands it back without saying a word about the alien overlord.

"Would you like to come to the party with me?"

Specs's eyes widen, and heat flares up my neck as I realize what I just said.

"I mean as a fake date," I add hastily. "Just pretend that you're with me. It'll give my parents the biggest shock of their lives. There's no way they won't notice me if I turn up with you on my arm."

"You mean… a big greasy biker?"

I've offended him. "No," I say quickly. "I just mean someone different from their world. Someone who's real. Someone who's not afraid to get a tattoo, and grow their facial hair, and wear leather because it looks good."

He chuckles. "You want your parents to notice you, huh?"

"Yeah. I want them to notice me this year. To know that I'm here."

I hold my breath, waiting for him to answer. I think about all the reasons this is a terrible idea.

Specs leans forward and puts the invite back on the

armrest. His hand creeps forward until it takes mine in his.

"I'll be your fake date, Cassie, if that's what you want. But I warn you, I'm going to make this the best fake date you've ever had."

4

CASSIE

My satin dress clings to my thighs as I pace the pavement in front of the vineyard where the party is being held. Specs said he'd meet me here, and my stomach is in knots as I await his arrival.

I have no idea what my parents will make of the big biker.

As I look at the fairy lights adorning the vineyard's courtyard and the elegant women arriving in SUVs with tinted windows, I wonder if I've made a mistake.

The roar of a bike has my stomach churning, and I clench my fists together on my sweaty palms. A Harley weaves its way through the line of SUVs.

The valet eyes the bike warily and speaks into his headset, no doubt warning security there might be trouble.

Specs pulls the bike into a small space, and I get to him just as the valet does.

"I'm sorry, sir, there is a private function on this evening."

I hasten forward and put a hand on Specs's leather-clad arm. "He's with me."

The valet gives me a curt nod. "Apologies, Miss Roper."

He turns to Specs, and if he has any doubts about the big biker, he doesn't show it. "Would you like me to park your bike for you?"

"Hell no." Specs slides off the Harley. "No one touches my girl."

As he says the words, his eyes dart to me, and a delicious shiver races down my spine.

The valet steps back to assist another arrival, and Specs's gaze remains on mine. He's trimmed his beard into a neat style, and the scent of masculine cologne reaches me. Heat pulses through my body, and my stomach does a double flip.

"I'm sorry about the valet. That was rude."

Specs shrugs. "That's what I'm here for, isn't it? To cause a stir?"

He's right. This is a fake date, I remind myself. Nothing more.

We head to the covered walkway that leads through to the terrace where the party is happening. Lanterns hang in the walkway, their soft light absorbed by the stone walls.

On the other side of the passageway is the hustle and bustle of the party. I hear the sound of glasses clinking, chatter, and high-pitched laughter.

I take a deep breath. My parents are in there with every single one of their business partners and associates. Am I really doing the right thing?

Specs stops before we get to the end of the passage and step into the light.

"Hey." He turns to face me. "I can leave if you want me to."

In the dim light, his face looks softer. His kind eyes peer at me, full of concern. Even if we weren't doing this for show, Specs is exactly who I want to be by my side.

"No," I say. "I invited you. Let's go to the party."

He takes my hand, and warmth shoots up my arm. "Let's do this."

We step out the other side of the walkway and into the party.

Soft light illuminates the paved area in front of us where guests mingle. Fairy lights run along every pathway, and torches blaze in iron torch holders.

A string quartet plays classical music, and the strains of a violin ring out across the vineyard. Beyond the paved area, the ground dips to a walled rose garden, and beyond that, the lines of grape vines fade into the darkness.

I take a deep breath as I scan the crowd, looking for my parents. People close to us stop and stare at Specs. Soon, the entire party is looking at us.

I tense. This is what I wanted, right? To make a scene. But I hate the attention on us.

Specs squeezes my hand. He doesn't look bothered at all, and that makes me mad. He should be bothered that these snobby assholes are staring at him because he looks different from them.

Instead, he nods toward the bar in the garden. "Let's get a drink."

He walks casually, and the crowd parts for him, eyeing his Wild Riders MC patch as we pass.

Ladies frown at me in disapproval. I hear the words whispered: "That's Cassie Roper. That's Ian and Lynn's daughter."

There are disapproving looks from the women, but not all of them. One woman, sucking on a cigarette with thick wrinkles around her eyes, looks Specs up and down and raises an eyebrow in appreciation. She winks at me and smiles, and I smile back at her. The gesture gives me confidence, and I square my shoulders and lift my chin.

Why shouldn't Specs be here? I was invited to the party, and he's my plus one.

I tilt my shoulders back and hold my head high.

We get to the bar, and Specs leans casually on the counter. If he's feeling self-conscious, he doesn't show it.

"What can I get you to drink, Cassie?"

I don't usually drink, but tonight I need something strong.

"Rum and Coke, please."

The bartender frowns at me. "You sure you wouldn't like some champagne or a cocktail?"

I'm about to change my order. It would be the right thing to do. But I'm tired of pretending with my parents. I've been the good daughter for so long I'm wearing a dress they would approve of. I'm here at their party. But I just want to be myself for once.

"No," I say firmly. "A Rum and Coke, please."

"Certainly." The bartender turns to Specs, and he rubs his beard.

"Don't suppose you serve beer at a party like this?"

The bartender motions to a fridge behind him. "Of course we do, sir. I've got some of the finest craft beers. I recommend this local one from the Wild Taste Brewery."

Specs chuckles. The Wild Taste Brewery is the brewery that the Wild Riders MC runs. I know he's thinking exactly what I am. If the vineyard is good enough to serve their beer, then why is everyone looking at him like he doesn't belong?

"I've heard that's good beer," he says with a chuckle.

The bartender takes a bottle from the fridge and slides a glass along the counter.

Specs holds up his hand. "I prefer drinking it from the bottle."

"Certainly."

The bartender hands over the bottle. Specs takes the beer and turns around to lean his elbows on the bar as he faces the party.

There's a tap on my shoulder, and I spin around to find my dad. He's got a smile plastered on his face, but his eyes burn with anger.

"Hello, Cassie. I didn't know you were bringing anyone."

I give him a bright smile. "This is Specs. He's my plus one."

My dad, aware that every eye in the vicinity is on him, offers a polite hand to shake.

"Specs. That's an unusual name."

Specs takes his hand and I tense, worried Dad is going to do something stupid like try to assert dominance with a power handshake. If he does, Specs doesn't show it.

"It's my road name," he says. "But you can call me Paul."

I glance around at Specs, or Paul. In the years I've known him, this is the first time I've learned his real name.

"Paul," I say softly, trying it out.

His eyes flick to mine, and something smolders in them.

"Cassie," my dad says. "Can I speak to you for a moment?"

Specs's look turns sharp. "Will you be okay?"

He's been playing it casual, but I can tell he's ready to protect me if I need it.

"Yeah," I say. "I'll be back in a minute."

Dad takes me by the arm, and his fingers dig into my forearm as he leads me a few steps away to a quiet part of the garden. He's smiling at people and saying hello as we walk past, but as soon as we're in the shadows, he drops my arm and the smile fades.

"What the hell are you doing, Cassie?"

I take a sip of my drink and feign innocence. "Enjoying the party."

"You know what I mean. Why did you bring a patched member of a motorcycle club to our party?"

His disapproval is like a pang to the heart. This is what I wanted, isn't it? I wanted to get my parents' attention. But now that I have it, it feels all wrong.

I wanted them to be shocked that I brought Specs along. But now that they are shocked, I'm angry. I'm angry that they can only see a biker. They don't see the man that he is.

"He's my date," I say, sticking my chin out.

"Since when are you dating?" Dad runs a hand through his hair. "This is Isabella's influence, isn't it? Ever since she married that biker, you've been running with a bad crowd."

I scoff. "If you mean a group of veterans who served this country, then yeah, I've been hanging out with them."

"He's a patched member of a motorcycle club, Cassie. He's wearing the jacket, and these are all our most important business partners. Don't you know how much this means to your mother and me?"

And there it is. The only thing my parents care about: their business.

Dad isn't concerned I might be hanging out with a bad crowd; he's concerned about how it reflects on his business.

"I'm sorry if your business associates are snobs, Dad, but if you want Paul to leave, you'll have to chuck him out."

Dad will never cause such a scene, and we both know it.

He glares at me, and I casually take a sip of my drink.

He glares at my tumbler, no doubt willing it to turn into an elegant champagne flute.

I swirl the ice around in the bottom of the glass and knock the drink back. It burns my throat, and I school my features so he doesn't notice.

He glances over to Specs, and I follow his gaze. Specs is leaning on the bar, deep in conversation with a man in a pale blue suit. He's also drinking a Wild Taste beer straight from the bottle.

It seems not everyone here is a snob like my parents.

Dad frowns and starts back toward the bar.

The man looks over as we approach and raises his beer bottle to dad. "I didn't know your daughter was so well connected."

Dad's eyes widen in surprise.

"Paul's the financial director for the Wild Taste Brewery." The man stares at his beer bottle thoughtfully. "His MC runs the place."

There's irritation behind Dad's eyes, but he hides it well.

"Is that so?" he says coolly.

The man sips his beer and smacks his lips. "We're looking to add craft beer to our offering. One of our big distributors in France is asking for it."

Specs nods sagely. I've never seen this side of him, the businessman. Whenever I've been at the club, he's either got his head in a spreadsheet, his bike engine, or a book.

"Here's my card." The man pulls a card out of his breast pocket and hands it to Specs. "Let's arrange a meeting."

"I'll have Quentin give you a call." Specs pockets the card. "He's the man to speak to."

The man offers his hand, and they shake.

I turn to my dad, whose smile is plastered on. My smile is genuine. Specs was meant to shock my parents, and he has, but I'm pleased not everyone is as judgy as my dad.

"Is that your Harley outside?" Another man comes up to Specs, and they get into a conversation about bikes.

Dad huffs away, and I order another drink. Specs was meant to shock, but he fits into my world easier than expected, except with my parents.

5
PAUL

*I*t's surprising how many bike enthusiasts are at this party and how they're flocking to me for advice because I'm wearing a leather jacket.

"She purrs like a kitten," a man in a dark blue suit jacket and a striped tie tells me. He waves his wine glass around. "I had the engine refitted and drove from Hope all the way to the Santa Rosa in California."

He launches into a story from his road trip, and I nod politely. My gaze shifts from the man, and as he tells me about the long desert roads, I scan the crowd for Cassie.

I miss her by my side. I've been aware of her all night. In her slinky dress that clings to her full figure, who wouldn't? She slipped away about twenty minutes ago to use the restroom, and I haven't seen her since.

I can't see her in the crowd near the bar, which is where we've stayed for the past hour.

"Excuse me." I cut the man off mid-sentence. "I have to find my date."

I leave him complaining about the state of the roads in California to the other guests who came to check me out, the curiosity at their swanky party.

I walk back to the entryway which is on higher ground and scan the crowd for Cassie. I can't see her among the guests. I catch her dad near the band. He has his arm around the waist of a thin woman with the same dark hair as Cassie who must be her mother.

Cassie isn't with them.

She's probably found a quiet corner somewhere to read. Although that dress doesn't have anywhere to stash a book. I should know; my gaze has roved over every inch of it.

I look past the crowd and to the garden. There's a lone figure strolling along an empty path in the rose garden. Cassie.

I head back through the crowd and past the bar. There's a cobblestone path that leads into the garden, and I take it. Fairy lights are strewn over the metal railings that line the path, with creeping roses growing up around them.

The noise of the party fades the further into the garden I go. I find Cassie by a water feature peering at the inscription on the stone fountain.

She startles when she sees me.

Her finger runs over the inscription. "It's a Shakespearean sonnet. "Shall I compare thee to a summer's day..."

"For thou art more lovely and more temperate," I finish with her.

Her eyes widen in surprise. "You know it?"

"I have a thing for classic literature. I was always getting told off at school for having my head in a book."

Cassie smiles. "Isn't that a good thing?"

"Not when you're in science class. I'd rather read poetry than learn the periodic table."

She wanders over toward me, her fingers trailing on the stone of the water feature.

"I needed some quiet. Being around people gets to be too much after a while."

I understand what she means. "Do you want me to leave you alone?"

She shakes her head. "Walk with me."

Four paths lead away from the water feature in different directions. Cassie chooses the one that leads away from the party, and I walk with her. The rose bushes turn to thick pivot bushes and there are no fairy lights this far from the party. Only the occasional gas light burns in an iron holder.

"If you like books so much, how did you get into accounting?" she asks.

It's a fair question. I do the accounts for the club and all the Wild Riders' businesses. "It's hard to earn a living from books."

Cassie stiffens. "You sound like my parents."

"It's what my mom said to me too. I joined the military because it brought in a regular paycheck. They discovered I had a head for figures, and instead of fighting on the front line I was put in the office. I learned accounting in the military. They paid for my education, and I gave them years of service in return. I never would have dreamed of getting a degree if it weren't for the military. Where I came from, people don't go to college."

"Why did you leave?"

"I did twelve years before my mom got sick. She's on her own, and it was hard on her. She fought the cancer and she's fine. Well, as fine as she'll ever be."

"You're close to your mom." Cassie sounds wistful, and I wonder at the strange relationship she has with her parents.

"I see her every week. She lives in Wild; I like to check in and make sure she's doing okay." I don't tell her where Mom lives exactly. Cassie has had a privileged upbringing. She grew up surrounded by vineyards and designer clothes and houses with more bathrooms than people.

"How about you? What do you want to do with your one beautiful life?"

She shrugs. "I'm studying business."

We walk in silence, and I'm aware of the swish of her skirt and how close we are.

"That didn't answer my question."

"It's stupid."

We turn down another path, and this one has a stone wall on one side. On the other is the dark vineyard. There's no light here, and I take Cassie's hand in mine. "Tell me."

She stops and turns to me. "Promise not to laugh."

"I promise."

She sucks in a deep breath, and then the words tumble out quickly. "I want to be a writer."

She bites her lower lip and looks down like it's something to be ashamed about.

"Hey," I slide my finger under her chin and tilt her head up. "That's nothing to be embarrassed about."

"My parents disagree."

"Do you do everything your parents tell you to?"

I take a step closer, and her eyes widen. Her thighs skim mine, and my heart thumps against my rib cage.

"No," she whispers.

"Maybe it's time to do something for yourself, Cassie."

My thumb brushes over her bottom lip, and I pull it down. Her lips are full and soft and so damned kissable.

"What is it you want to write?" I trail my fingers down her throat, and she tilts her head back. "If there was no judgement from your parents. What is it you want?"

My fingers rest on her neck, and her pulse races under my touch. I squeeze her neck slightly, and she gasps. "I want to write romance."

My hand slides down her body and clutches her waist. I step her backwards until she's leaning against the wall.

My lips press to her throat, and her pulse beats against my lips.

"Is this okay?' I ask. "Is this something you want?"

She nods. "Yes."

"Good. Because from now on you're going to stop pleasing others, Cassie, and you're going to do exactly what you want. You understand?"

She nods, and my hands slide down her thighs. I duck

down until my fingers grip the bottom of her dress. Slowly, I tug the slick fabric up while trailing my fingers over the smooth skin on her calves, then upward to her thighs.

"If I'm doing something you don't want to do, you tell me, okay?"

She whimpers as I skim the soft skin of her inner thighs. Heat radiates from her center, and my dick hardens as my fingers linger on the apex of her thighs.

My other hand keeps her pinned to the wall. "Tell me, Cassie. Is this what you want?"

"Yes," she whimpers.

"Yes what? Tell me exactly what you want."

My fingertips brush her panties, and Cassie moans. My body is electrified at the sound, and my dick twitches to attention.

"I want you to touch me, Paul."

"Good girl." My fingers stroke her panties and come away wet. "Now tell me. Be honest. What do you want to do with your life?"

Her brow furrows as my strokes set a steady rhythm.

"I…"

"Tell me, Cassie."

"I want to be a writer. I want to tell stories."

"Good girl." I slide my hands into the top of her panties, and she gasps as I grip her mound. She's soaking wet, and my fingers get coated in her juice.

"What kind of stories?" I pull my hand back, waiting for her to answer.

"I…" Her gaze flicks to mine, and there's desire in her eyes and hunger. "Please, Paul."

She squirms against the wall and her hips move forward, but I keep my hand hovering just over her.

"What kind of writer do you want to be, Cassie? Tell me and I'll make you feel good. I'll give you the release you need, baby."

She bites her lower lip. "I want to write romance."

"Good girl." I press my palm to her needy pussy, and she whimpers as I move in slow circles.

I kiss her neck and throat and let her have a few moments of pleasure. But she hasn't told me everything, and I want to get a confession out of her. I want Cassie to admit to the things she wants and then go after them.

The sounds of the party can be heard in the distance, but the only noises I'm tuned into are the whimpers and moans as Cassie dances on the palm of my hand.

While my palm circles her clit, I bring my middle finger to circle her soft entrance. I tease her with the tip, and her moans turn to little cries.

I pull away, and her eyes fly open. I chuckle at the frustration and need in her expression.

"You're holding back, Cassie."

"I'm not. Please…"

"What kind of romance do you want to write?"

She jerks forward and grabs my hand and thrusts it toward her. I love her determination, and I reward her with gentle strokes.

"Tell me, Cassie. Tell me what you want to do, what

you really want to write. Release it to me, and I'll release you."

She huffs in frustration, and I still my hand.

Cassie screws her face up tight and closes her eyes. "Alien romance. I want to write alien romance."

"Good girl." I thrust my finger into her. She cries out as I impale her on my hand. She leans forward, gripping my shoulders.

"Good girl, Cassie. You're a good girl," I whisper in her ear.

She moans and turns her face toward mine. My lips find hers, and I kiss her hard. My fingers slide deeper and I let her lose herself, kissing and stroking and thrusting until she comes undone on the palm of my hand.

Her cries echo around the dark garden and are carried over the vineyard. She stills on my hand, and her eyes flicker open.

"I've never done that before," she whispers.

"You've never come?"

She shakes her head. "I've come loads of times."

Jealousy flares in my chest, instant and harsh. My body tenses. I can't bear the thought of Cassie with another man.

"By myself," she adds shyly.

The jealousy abates. "You've never been with a man?"

She shakes her head. "I'm a virgin." She looks down. "But I think I'd like to…" She trails off.

"What Cassie?" I growl. "Say what you want."

"I'd like you to be the one, to, you know…take my virginity."

I growl, and my lips clash into hers. My hand moves against her pussy. I'll take her virginity, but that's not all I want. I want Cassie's heart, and until she belongs to me, I won't claim her that way.

But I will give her one hell of a fake date to remember.

My hand moves slowly, and it doesn't take long to bring her to another orgasm. Then another.

It's only after she collapses against me, exhausted, that I release her.

There's a bench on the other side of the wall, and we sit for a while and she leans against me.

"You won't tell anyone, will you?"

"About this? Hell no. This is between you and me."

"I mean about the alien romance."

I turn to her. "I'll make you a deal. I won't tell anyone as long as you start writing your first book."

Her eyes widen. "No. I couldn't. It's a stupid idea. I don't know where to begin…"

I raise my eyebrows and wait.

She chews her bottom lip. "I mean, I've got ideas. I've scribbled notes and some bits of scenes. But I don't know how to write a book, and then how do you get it published?"

I bring a finger to her lips.

"Just start at the beginning and write your story. If you want to publish it, we'll figure that out, but write the book you want to write, Cassie."

6

CASSIE

*M*orning sunlight streams through my bedroom windows, casting luminous patterns on my bedroom walls. I stretch lazily and roll over to face the light, letting it warm me in its glow. But it's not just the sunlight that makes my body heat. Memories of what we did in the garden flood my mind.

Paul's hands on me and the confession he extracted from me as well as the release. I've never told anyone my ambitions to write alien romance. Whenever I mentioned wanting to be a writer to my parents, their eyes glazed over. They insisted I study business in college and I stupidly went along with them, believing them when they told me it would set me up for the future. But the future my parents want for me is different from what I want for myself.

Paul made me realize that last night. And it's not just the writing. I want him. I want his hands on me; I want to feel his beard tickle my throat. I want to feel what it's like to make love to the gentle biker with rough hands.

A knock on my door has me sitting up in bed and wrapping the comforter around my shoulders.

Dad barges in before I have time to ask who it is. The expression on his face tells me everything I need to know.

"Morning!" I say cheerfully.

His eyebrows are pulled together, and his mouth is set in a thin line. "What kind of stunt were you pulling last night?"

My cheeks heat. For a moment I think he's talking about what Paul and I did in the garden. Perhaps a guest saw us and reported back to my parents.

"What do you mean?" I keep my voice calm, trying to gauge what Dad knows.

"Bringing a patched member of a biker gang to our party."

Relief floods me, and I lean back on the pillows. Dad doesn't know about our tryst in the garden. He's just hung up about Paul.

"He seemed to be a hit," I reply. "He collected three business cards, brokered a deal for distributing the Wild Taste craft beer in Europe, and booked two bikes at their repair shop."

Dad's frown deepens. "It's a party, not a networking opportunity for the local MC."

I scoff at his words. "Aren't those parties one big networking opportunity?"

I'll bet any money that both Mom and Dad had a hit list of important guests they wanted to speak to and a plan of who would speak to whom.

He folds his arms across his chest. "They are an opportunity to get to know our business associates in a casual environment."

"Sounds like networking to me." I slide out of bed and pull my robe over my pajamas.

Dad scowls at me. "You know how important these functions are to your mother and me."

I know they're more important than their own daughter. Anger flares inside me, and I tie the belt of my robe too tight.

"You missed my birthday."

Dad looks confused for a moment, then his expression softens. "Ah, I'm sorry, Cassie. It was last week, wasn't it?"

"Yes. You and Mom forgot because you were too busy planning your precious party."

He strides over and puts a hand on my shoulder. "I'm sorry, Cassie. We'll make it up to you. We'll go to dinner tonight at the restaurant you like in Hope." He frowns. "Not tonight, actually. I've got a late meeting. We'll go Friday."

"Isn't Mom on a business trip on Friday?"

I keep track of my parents better than they keep a track of me. It's not that hard. Their assistant sends me their schedule so I know where they are.

"Ah yes." Dad frowns. "She's going to visit a supplier in the Napa Valley. How about next week?"

Next week will be three weeks after my birthday. My best friend managed to put on a party for me despite having a toddler and a difficult pregnancy. My parents have to wait three weeks to celebrate my birthday.

"Don't worry about it, Dad. My friends already celebrated with me." I can't keep the bitterness out of my voice. "My friends at the MC."

The scowl returns to his face. "Is that why you brought that…man to the party? Because we forgot your birthday? It worked, Cassie. You have our attention."

It was the original reason I invited Specs, but we had such a good time together. He was attentive and funny and interesting to talk to. And he can do wicked things with his hands. Bringing Specs to the party was a way to get my parents' attention, but now I just want his attention.

"No," I say. "I invited him because I like him."

My father's expression turns thunderous. "He's in a motorcycle club, Cassie. He wears a patched jacket and has numerous tattoos."

"Yes." I stick my chin out. "He also served for twelve years in the military, is a certified accountant, and runs all the finances for the various legitimate businesses the club owns. He's kind and funny and loves books. If you could see past your own ass, you'd see that he's a nice guy."

My dad's eyes widen. I've never spoken to him like that before, and I regret the disrespectful tone as soon as I've used it.

"You never used to speak like this, Cassie."

"How would you know? You're never around. You're too busy planning parties and schmoozing with your business associates."

He shakes his head. "The business relationships we have are what pays for this house, your nice clothes, and that college degree you've got."

He clenches his fist, and a vein throbs in his neck. "As long as you're under this roof that your mother and I pay for, you live by my rules. And I forbid you from seeing that man again."

The air goes out of my lungs. I've never seen my dad so angry. But he's being unreasonable.

If I have to choose between living with my parents, who don't notice me, and Specs who makes me feel seen, then the choice is easy.

"Fine." I fold my arms over my chest and school my expression to neutral. I don't want Dad to get a hint of what I'm about to do or he might try to stop me.

His eyes narrow, and I don't think he believes he won the argument that easily. He's about to say something when his phone rings.

He looks at the screen. "I have to take this."

Of course he does. It's a business call, and despite being a Saturday morning, his business associates mean everything to him.

"But we're not done here." He glares at me before leaving the room. I hear his voice fade down the corridor as he takes the call.

My father's given me an ultimatum, and there's only one choice.

I pull out my small backpack from my wardrobe. I need to pack light, only what I can take on the back of a motorbike.

PAUL

I take the mountain bends quicker than I should on my way to get to Cassie. She called twenty minutes ago in tears. I couldn't get the whole story out of her, but I got the message; she needs me.

Cassie's waiting outside the gates when I pull up to her place. She's clutching a small rucksack to her chest that's bursting at the seams and has a laptop bag slung over her shoulder.

I pull up beside her and slide off the bike.

"Are you okay? Are you hurt?"

"I'm fine. But please…" She glances furtively behind her. "Get me out of here."

I've got so many questions, but there's an urgency to her voice, and the way she glances behind her makes me think her parents wouldn't be happy to know I'm here stealing away their daughter.

"Will these fit in your saddlebag? I didn't know how much I could take."

She hands me her laptop bag and rucksack, which is heavier than I expected. I open the saddlebag and slide her laptop bag in, then try to cram in the rucksack. There's not much give in it.

"What you got in here?"

She looks at me sheepishly. "Books."

Of course it's books. I don't question her. I just shuffle the weight around until I make it all fit.

She's wearing a thick sweater, but it's a cold day and it won't be enough.

I take my jacket off. "You're going to need to wear this."

Cassie slides my jacket on, and I love how she looks wearing my cut. I hand her my spare helmet and make sure it's clicked on properly before getting on the bike.

"Please, let's just go," she says.

I rev up the engine, and we head down the mountain. Cassie clings onto me, her small fingers tight around my waist. Something's troubling her, and I'll protect her in any way she needs me to. But I need to know what I'm protecting her from.

This side of the mountain looks out over the Hope Valley with the town of Hope in the distance. Mansions dot the landscape, and we pass the occasional driveway leading down to a house as big as her parents' with views just as good. This is the high-end side of the mountain, and the road rushes past beneath us as we leave it behind.

Another twenty minutes and we drive through Wild with its one pub and convenience store, a world away from the mansions on Cassie's side of the mountain.

My instinct is to take her to the club headquarters. She'll be safe there. But I don't know what the situation is, and knowing Cassie, she won't like to be around people. Instead, I take her to a lookout spot. It's down a gravel road, so no one will see my bike if her parents come looking for her.

We park, and I turn to her on the bike. "Let's sit for a while and look at the view."

She slides her helmet off, and we walk over to the boulders that sit to one side of a small picnic area. We climb up and sit next to each other, looking out at the valley below us.

It's a long, comfortable silence. I never feel the need to talk when I'm with Cassie. I think she feels the same.

Our thighs bump together, and heat shoots through my veins. The memory of kissing her and touching her and making her come undone floods my brain.

But I put all those thoughts aside because right now, I need to know what's going on with my girl.

"What do you need, Cassie?" I ask. "I'm here for you. I will take care of you. I will protect you in any way you need. Just tell me what it is."

She plays with the zipper on my jacket. "I don't want to go back there."

"Why? Did something happen?" My fists clench. I don't know how bad the situation is with her parents, but if they laid a finger on her, I'll go back there and make them pay.

"No," she says. "Nothing bad." She sighs. "I just... I don't want to live there anymore."

I unclench my fists and let out a long breath. If they're not physically hurting her, then it must be something they said.

"Did your parents say something?"

She presses her lips together and looks out at the view.

"I've just had enough. I'm twenty-three years old. It's time I stood on my own two feet."

There's something she's not telling me, but I don't push. The best thing I can do for Cassie right now is to be here for her, however she needs me.

"I don't want to live there anymore, but I don't have anywhere else to go."

I take her hand in mine, and she looks up at me. Her eyes are wide and troubled, and I want to ease that pain for her.

"Of course you have somewhere to go, Cassie. You can come stay with me."

Something flickers over her face, and I wonder if I'm moving too fast. Maybe last night was a one-off for her. Maybe she just wanted a quick fumble with the rough biker boy.

But when I look into her wide eyes, I'm sure that's not the case.

"Last night was... incredible," I say. "And if you want to do that again, we can. But if you don't want to, there's no pressure, Cassie."

It seems Cassie's spent her life doing what her parents have wanted. I want to help her find what it is she wants. I just hope that's me.

"I can tell you what I want. I want you to come stay with me at my cabin as my woman."

She sucks in a breath.

"But if you're not ready for that, you can stay as my friend."

I should take her to the club headquarters. We've got spare rooms, and they're used often by women who need somewhere to stay. But I'm a selfish bastard, and I want to keep her to myself.

"I can't give you the same comfort you're used to, Cassie. My cabin is small. I don't have a butler or a cleaner or separate bathrooms, but you're welcome to stay."

She smiles and squeezes my hand. "It sounds perfect."

She's perfect. That's what I want to tell her. But I don't want to scare her right now. She needs a sanctuary, and I can be that for her.

There's plenty of time for her to realize she belongs to me.

8

CASSIE

*A*s I cling to the back of Specs on the motorbike, the anxiety in my stomach slowly slips away.

We had one night making out, and here I am throwing myself at him and asking to stay. But despite the imposition, he's calm and understanding and sincere.

His words echo around my brain. He wants me to be his woman, but he's leaving it up to me. I press against him, and his warmth and the whir of the motorbike calms my mind. I don't know what I want, but right now, in this moment, being on the back of Specs's bike feels damn good.

We turn off the main road down a gravel road. Thick trees line the narrow path and grow so close together that only narrow shafts of sunlight break through.

The bike slows as we get to the end of the path, and I realize this is Specs's driveway. We come out into a clearing, and a neat wooden cabin squats in the middle.

The cabin is dwarfed by the giant sycamore trees

surrounding it. A wooden porch runs around the outside of the cabin, and a single rocking chair sits next to a small wooden table. Large ceramic pots line the wall, and as we walk up the stairs to the door, I breathe in the scents of sage, rosemary, and lavender.

"It's an herb garden," I murmur. "I didn't know you were into gardening."

Specs chuckles. "I'm into cooking. And you can't beat having fresh herbs at your doorstep."

He unlocks the door and holds it open for me to step inside.

The inside of the cabin smells like baked bread and a mixture of herbs. On the kitchen counter sits a fresh loaf of bread, still in its pan.

"I was baking when I got your call," Specs says. "It had just come out of the oven, and I didn't have time to turn it out."

He moves over to the kitchen and pulls a cooling rack from a cupboard and expertly tips the loaf upside down. It plops onto the rack, and a fresh wave of baked-bread aroma fills the air.

My stomach rumbles at the smell. "I didn't know you baked."

Specs chuckles. "I like food. I like to cook and bake and read and tinker with bikes. They're my hobbies."

He grins, and it lights up his entire face

"You like scrambled eggs? I'll make us lunch." He comes alive in his kitchen and moves with a confidence that's magnetic, producing a bowl and taking eggs from the pantry.

"Eggs sound good."

"Make yourself at home." He waves a whisk in the air to indicate the rest of the cabin.

I turn around, and my breath catches in my throat.

The cabin is open plan with the kitchen joined to the living area. A wood burner sits against one wall, and on the adjacent wall is a floor-to-ceiling bookcase. Opposite the wood burner is an armchair with a knitted blanket thrown over the arm and a cushion squished into the back of it. It's obvious this is where Specs sits. Next to the armchair is a small coffee table with a coaster and a book. There's another armchair on the other side of the table.

I clasp my hands together. "This is perfect."

Specs looks up from whisking the eggs. "It's not much, but it's home."

"Not much?" It's a book lover's dream. "It's so cozy."

He chuckles. "Cozy's one word for it. It's small. I don't have a lot of company."

I turn around, suddenly aware of taking up his space. "I'm intruding. I'm sorry. I can call Isabella…"

Specs waves a hand dismissively. "I wouldn't have invited you if I didn't want you here. Isabella's busy with the toddler, and the pregnancy…"

He doesn't finish the sentence. He doesn't have to. I know how sick my friend's been with this pregnancy. That's why I didn't call her. Well, it's one of the reasons.

"You want one egg or two?" he calls from the kitchen.

"I'll have two, please."

51

"This won't take me long. Make yourself comfortable."

I wander over to the bookcase and let my fingers drift over the spines. He's arranged them alphabetically by author. I arrange mine by the colors of the spine.

I pull out a copy of *Emma* by Jane Austen.

"You read Jane Austen?"

Specs shrugs. "I read everything. It's a classic. I much prefer *Pride and Prejudice*."

The fact that he reads Jane Austen make my chest squeeze. If I'm not careful, I could seriously fall for this man.

"*Pride and Prejudice* is my favorite too. I can relate to Elizabeth more than any of her other heroines. And you can't beat Darcy," I add. "A classic hero. The original book boyfriend."

Specs frowns a little, and if I didn't know any better, I'd think he was jealous.

"If you like that kind of thing," he mumbles. "Bit too privileged for my liking."

I take the copy of *Emma* and get comfy in the spare armchair. It's an old version with thick brown paper and a tattered dust jacket. I open it carefully and begin to read.

We sit at the kitchen counter on barstools for lunch. The homemade bread is delicious, and the scrambled eggs have a handful of herbs mixed through.

"These are fresh eggs from my chooks out back," he says. "My girls keep me company."

"I love that you've got chickens."

"What can I tell you? I'm a simple man. I like simple things." He frowns. "I'm sorry it's not what you're used to."

I set my fork down to look at him. "Paul, this is perfect. I love it. But... have you got room for me to stay?"

He put his hand over mine. "Of course there is, Cassie. You take the bed. There's only one bedroom, but it's yours."

"Where will you sleep?" I glance around at the tiny living room with the two armchairs. There's not even a couch.

"That's a lazy boy," he says, indicating the armchair by the bookcase. "I've dozed in that more than once."

"I can't kick you out of your bed."

He shakes his head. "You're not kicking me out, Cassie. You're my guest. You need a place to stay. You take the bed. It's yours for as long as you need it."

He squeezes my hand, and heat prickles up my arm.

What I want to do is invite him into the bed with me. I want to repeat what we did last night. But I'm not experienced with men.

"Do you have things to do today?" I ask. "I'm sorry I'm ruining your Saturday."

He shakes his head. "No plans. I'm here for you today, Cassie. Whatever you want to do."

I glance at the bookcase and the comfy armchairs. "Could we stay here and read?"

A huge grin spreads across his face. "That sounds like the perfect day."

Paul clears up the dishes and makes us both a pot of

coffee. He brings my bags in from the back of his bike, and I pull out my books and my eReader.

"It would have been easier if you'd just bought your eReader." He indicates the stack of hardcovers I pull out of my bag.

I stare at him in disbelief. "I couldn't leave these behind! Look how pretty they are, my special edition hardcovers."

I hold up the three books in the series and show him the pattern they make when all the spines are lined up together.

Specs nods. "I see." There's not a hint of sarcasm in his voice; he really does get it. "Let me clear some space for you."

He takes out some books from his bookshelf. "You're not getting rid of those, are you?"

Specs looks sheepish. "I've got another bookcase in the bedroom. Don't worry. We've got space for books."

It's an oddly touching gesture. I slide my hardbacks into the space on the bookshelf and wonder what it would be like to live in a place like this, without the trappings of the huge house. Just books, a fire, chickens, an herb garden—and Specs.

He brings over two mugs of steaming coffee. Then he goes into the bedroom and comes back with a blanket.

But instead of settling with a book, I pull my laptop out of my bag. Being here in this cozy cabin with Paul is inspiring.

Paul raises an eyebrow.

"After the party last night, I was so inspired I started plotting the first book."

He grins at me. "Cassie, that's awesome."

"I've never told anyone that's what I want to do before. You don't think it's stupid, do you?"

He cups my cheek in his hand. "I think it would be stupid not to follow your dreams. Write the book, Cassie. I believe in you."

9

CASSIE

I have written the first chapter of a book! I'm so freaking proud of myself. I can't stop the grin that's plastered on my face.

I look up from my laptop, and the light has faded outside. At some point in the afternoon, Paul put the fire on, and the entire cabin is lit up with a warm glow. He's back in the kitchen, humming as he makes dinner. He's been back and forth getting herbs from his garden, and the smells coming from the kitchen are delicious.

I put my laptop on the coffee table and stretch. I can't believe I've written the first few scenes of a book. It's a mess. It needs heavy editing, and I'm not quite sure if the hero's going to be blue or have a green tinge to his scaly skin. But I've done it. The first chapter is written.

"Can I help with anything?"

Paul looks up as I come into the kitchen. "Nah, I'm good. You just keep writing."

I take a seat on the counter and watch him expertly

dice up onions with a sharp knife. "I wrote the first chapter."

"Oh yeah?" His grin is as wide as mine. "That's great, Cassie."

"I just need to figure out how he gets her off Earth and to his planet."

He nods, his eyebrows pulling together. "Maybe his minions come and get her for him?"

I love that he's taking this as seriously as I am.

"I want him to come himself. Like, he instantly sees her, and then that's it, he has to have her."

Paul nods. "I'm sure you'll figure it out."

He slides a glass of orange juice over to me and I take a sip, still thinking about my story.

"I think I've got an idea." I slide off the barstool before realizing it might be rude to expect him to cook while I write. "Do you mind?"

He shakes his head. "You keep writing. I'll let you know when dinner's ready."

I go back to my laptop and type up a few notes, then get going on the next chapter. It feels like no time at all when Paul puts two plates down on the kitchen counter.

"Do you want this now, or do you want to keep working?"

I shake my head. "I'll stop."

It feels great to have written. I feel bold. I feel confident, like maybe I can do this. Maybe all I needed was to get out of my parents' house.

Paul has made Bolognese, and it's delicious. The sauce

is thick and tasty with all the herbs he's put into it. I curl the pasta around my fork.

"It's homemade pasta," he says.

My eyebrows shoot up my forehead. This man is full of surprises. "You can make it yourself?"

Paul chuckles. "Yeah, it's really easy. I do a batch at the start of the week and it lasts all week. I like making things from scratch."

There's a lot I'm learning about this quiet biker, and all of it makes me fall for him a little more. He is not what you'd expect a veteran member of an MC to be like.

"I can't imagine you in the military. What did you do?"

Paul pauses with his fork halfway to his mouth. "I was a financial manager. There's a lot of support staff that work in the site office. I didn't have the glamor of running out and shooting bad guys, but it suited me fine."

I imagine Paul in his military gear sitting in a heated office with a paperback stuffed in his pocket.

"I started like everyone else in basic training, but they saw something in me and trained me in accountancy. I'm grateful for that."

He looks away and smiles when he talks about the military. It was obviously a good part of his life, which makes me wonder why he's not still there.

"Why did you come out?"

Paul twirls pasta around his fork. "My mom got sick."

"I'm sorry to hear that," I say quietly.

"She beat the cancer. My mom's a tough old bird." He pops the forkful of pasta in his mouth and chews thoughtfully before swallowing. "I'm going to see her tomorrow. Would you like to come?"

I look down at my plate. I hate meeting new people, but it's an honor to be invited, and I'm curious about Paul's family.

"Yeah. I'd like that."

He beams at me, and I'm glad I've made him happy.

After dinner we clear up the dishes and then settle down to read quietly in the armchairs.

The only sound is the crackling of the fire and the wind outside as the trees scrape against the windows. Paul thought I wouldn't like the coziness of it, but the truth is, I love it here. It's peaceful and inspiring.

While Paul reads, I open my laptop. It's amazing how the words flow out of me now. My fingers fly over the keys. An hour passes, and I've written two more chapters. I close the laptop, suddenly tired.

Paul looks at me carefully. "You need to rest. I'll show you your room."

He stands and I follow him through the door. The short hallway leads to a bedroom on the left and a bathroom to the right, with cupboard space at the end.

The bedroom houses another floor-to-ceiling bookshelf. Pillows are propped up on the double bed, and a reading lamp is clamped to the headboard.

"I love your cabin, Paul," I say.

"It's not much, but it's home." He heads out the door to the cupboard at the end of the short hallway. "I'll get you a towel if you want to shower."

He comes back with a towel and puts it on the bed at

the same time that I reach for it. Our hands brush, and a spark of heat shoots up my arm. Our eyes lock, and heat sparks between us. HIs gaze flicks to my lips as he leans toward me Then his lips meet mine in a gentle kiss.

Memories of his hands on me make my body heat, and I want that again.

I lean toward Paul and twist my hips so they push against him. I'm feeling bold. I'm feeling confident. I just wrote two freaking chapters of a book; I can do anything.

My hands trail down his shirt and over his hard muscles. His hands tangle in my hair, and the kiss turns urgent and hungry.

Paul is being so good to me, and I want to return the favor.

My fingers drag down the front of his jeans and over the hard bulge there. As I slowly drop to my knees, my hands caress his thighs.

"Hey, what are you doing?"

I bite my lower lip, looking up at him as I slide my fingers under his belt.

"I want to make you feel as good as you made me feel last night."

Paul groans, and it's a low sexy rumble in his throat that makes me wet between the legs.

"You don't have to do that, Cassie."

My hand slides into his jeans and around the back, and I tug them down over his buttocks.

"I know." There's a patch of dampness on his boxers

right at the end of the bulge of his hard cock. I lean in and kiss it. "But I want to."

My hand slides into his boxers, and I slide them down his hips. His cock pops out, pointing straight at me, thick, long, and hard.

I keep my breathing steady. I've never done this before. I've never been so bold. But Paul makes me feel like I can do anything.

I press my lips to the throbbing cock in front of me.

Paul lets out a guttural sound in his throat, and that emboldens me. My tongue flicks out and licks from shaft to tip, tasting his saltiness. My mouth encloses the head of his cock.

He groans, an animalistic noise that sends heat between my legs. I want to make him make those sounds forever.

I've never done this before, so I go on instinct. One hand clasps the base of his shaft as I take him into my mouth, as far down as I can manage. His dick hits the back of my throat, and I gag.

His hands tangle in my hair, and he pulls my head back. "Hey, go easy. You can stop anytime you want."

I answer with my eyes locked on his, licking the tip of his cock like a lollipop. Paul groans, and his eyes roll back into his head.

I slide my mouth down his hard cock, my hands meeting in the middle, one on his shaft, one guiding him into my mouth. I try to keep my teeth out of the way, and use my tongue and lips to bring him pleasure slowly. I know he's enjoying it by the groans he makes and the way his hips thrust forward.

"Fuck…" he mumbles, moaning, my name on his lips. It makes me even wetter between the legs.

"Touch yourself, Cassie."

With his dick in my mouth and one hand on his shaft, I glide my other hand over my breasts. His eyes follow the path of my fingers as I tug on my nipples through my top, then move down my belly to the place between my legs. I spread my thighs and slide my hand into my pants.

The sensation of my fingers on my hard nub makes me moan in pleasure and spurs me on to make my mouth work harder. I suck and stroke him as my fingers circle my clit in tight, teasing spirals.

His fingers grip my hand, guiding it down his cock. I fight the gag reflex, taking him deeper and deeper.

With every thrust, I move my fingers faster until I can't stand it anymore.

I come. Hard.

The sounds I make are muffled by his cock in my mouth. I suck as hard as I can, and he explodes in my mouth, hot, sticky liquid hitting the back of my throat. I suck and suck, eager to get every last drop as my pussy throbs and my orgasm trembles through my body.

Only when I've swallowed every last piece of him do I slide him out of my mouth and sit back on my thighs, panting hard.

But I'm not satisfied. I won't be satisfied until I feel him inside me.

Paul lifts me up, spins me around, and sits me on the bed. He takes off my leggings and my panties.

"That was amazing. You're amazing," he says, kissing my mouth and my neck. He peels my shirt off and cups my breasts. His mouth finds my nipple and pulls it into his mouth as his other hand slides between my legs.

My pussy, still throbbing from the orgasm, responds instantly to his touch.

I lift my hips to meet his palm and he applies slow, steady circles until I'm writhing on the bed and crying out. Another orgasm races through me. And it leaves me panting and needing more.

"Paul…" My voice comes out a whimper. "Take my virginity."

He groans and his hand moves, tracing small, perfect circles on my clit.

"Not yet, Cassie. You're feeling bold, and I love that. But I won't claim you properly until I know you're mine. Body and soul."

As he speaks, his mouth moves down my body, planting kisses on my belly and trailing over my skin, lower and lower until he kisses my most sensitive parts.

I gasp at the sensation and throw my legs into the air. He hooks them around his shoulders and closes his mouth on my pussy. He applies pressure with his tongue, and the sensation is so strong that I grab the bedsheets and cry out his name.

One hand cradles my ass, lifting my hips up. His tongue dips into me while his lips massage my clit. The pressure builds again, and I scream his name as I let out another release. Then again, and again. His mouth is relentless. He brings me to peak after peak until I'm shuddering and breathless, lying on the bed with my body trembling and useless.

Only then does he release my legs and slip out from between my thighs.

I barely register it when he slips into the bathroom. I hear running water, and then he returns with a warm flannel and gently cleans my thighs, wiping away my sticky juices.

"Thank you," I mumble.

He pulls a T-shirt from his drawer, and I slip into it. I'm so tired I don't protest as he tucks the covers around me.

"Stay with me." I clasp him around the arm, needing to feel his solidness.

"Of course, Cassie. I'll stay with you, always."

He shucks off the rest of his clothes and climbs into bed beside me. I fall asleep with his arms wrapped around me, exactly where I want to be.

10

CASSIE

*P*aul is already up when I wake the next morning. Heat flushes my cheeks as I think about what we did together last night. I've never done anything like that before, and I wonder if things will be different between us now.

I take my time dressing, worried that as soon as I face Paul, the spell from last night will be broken.

There's a delicious smell coming from the kitchen, and the rumbling of my belly draws me out of the room.

"Morning, beautiful."

He smiles when he sees me, and my anxiety slips away. He's the same guy he was twenty-four hours ago. Nothing's changed. A mixing bowl sits in the kitchen sink, and other baking equipment lies scattered over the counter.

"Do you ever stop cooking?" I tease as he pulls a tray of scones out of the oven.

Paul chuckles. "I like to bake on the weekend. I always take my mom something."

My heart squeezes for the man who takes care of his mother so well.

"Do you still want to come visit her?" He's watching me carefully. This is a big deal for him, and he's waiting to see if I'll keep my word.

"Of course. If you don't mind me tagging along."

He shakes his head. "You're not tagging along, Cassie. I want you to meet her."

An hour later, I cling onto the back of Paul's bike as we drive into Wild. He stops outside the local convenience store and kills the engine.

"I just need to grab a few things."

I go in with him, and he fills a basket with canned food, fresh bread, baby formula, and diapers.

"Is this something you're not telling me?" I joke. "Have you got a secret baby hidden somewhere?"

He just smiles. "It's not for me."

He pays for the groceries and stuffs them into his saddlebag. Then we take the road behind the store, heading past run-down apartments into a residential area. We slow down as we ride past houses with overgrown grass and gates that hang off fences.

At the end of the road is a trailer park, and we turn in and stop by the reception desk.

A woman shuffles out of the office and raises a hand in greeting.

"Hey Paul." Her voice is croaky from age.

He greets the woman, and they chat for a few minutes as he pulls the groceries out of his saddle bag.

"This is for whoever needs it this week." He hands over the groceries, the diapers, and the large can of baby formula.

"God bless you," she says.

My chest expands as I watch Paul talk to the woman. He gets back on the bike, and my arms slide around his waist. We take the gravel path that weaves between the trailers slowly, but I hang on to him tight.

We dodge kids kicking a worn soccer ball around. Some of them chase the bike, and Paul reaches into his pocket and throws a bag of sweets back to them.

A man watering a line of plants outside a run-down trailer raises a hand in greeting.

They know him here, and adults and kids alike call out greetings as we ride past.

In the back corner of the park, we stop in front of a weather-stained trailer that's smaller than the rest. The wheels have been removed, and it's sitting on bricks. The brown paneling is worn in places, and one of the windows has a crack in it. Grass grows up around the base, and there's a canvas overhang that forms an awning over the door. Under the awning are a cluster of paving stones surrounded by colorful plant pots to form a small court-yard that encloses a plastic table and two plastic chairs.

At the sound of the bike, a woman comes to the door and leans on the doorframe as she watches us park.

Her gray hair is cut short, and deep wrinkles line her

eyes. She holds a cigarette in one hand, and ash falls to the soil as she taps it against the side of a pot plant.

"Morning, Paulie."

Her gaze moves to me, and her eyes light up with the same sparkle as her son's. "You brought a girl."

I slide off the bike, my stomach knotting. I've never been great at meeting new people, especially someone I want to impress, like Paul's mom.

"Let me have a look at you." She stubs out her cigarette in a potted plant and shuffles down the pathway. She takes my hands in her boney ones. Her fingers are stained yellow and crinkly like paper, lined from age and years of smoking.

"This is Cassie," Paul says. "This is Donna, my mom."

Donna squeezes my hands. "She's pretty, Paulie." She smiles at me. "And I bet you're smart too. You look smart." Her smile is infectious and I smile back at her, unsure what to say.

"Welcome to my home, Cassie." She releases her grip and her arm sweeps around, taking in the trailer and the small patch of paving stones and potted plants that make up her garden. "It's not much, but it's home."

There's pride in her voice as she surveys her small patch of the world. It makes me feel foolish for the mansion I live in. I've never heard my parents speak about our home that way.

"You two take a seat. I'll get the coffee."

I take one of the plastic chairs under the canopy. Paul ducks into the trailer and comes back with another chair that he places around the plastic table.

"How long has your mom lived here?" I ask. The potted plants are well cared for, and there are herbs among the flowers, their fragrance tinged with the smell of cigarettes.

"She moved in after she got sick." He pulls on his beard. "I grew up somewhere similar but further down the mountain."

A soccer ball bounces on the paving stones and bumps into the leg of the table, then rolls toward Paul. He kicks it back to the kid who comes looking for it.

"Thanks Paul," the boy shouts as he runs off with his friends.

I wonder what it would it be like to grow up in a place like this. Suddenly, the privilege I grew up with hits me. Just a short way up the mountain, I'm living in a mansion, and people here are scratching out an existence in a trailer park.

"Do you take sugar?" Donna sets mismatched mugs on the table and comes back with the pot of coffee and a carton of milk. She pours out the coffee and takes a seat.

Paul takes the container of scones out of his saddlebag, and Donna ducks inside to get plates.

I talk easily with his mom. Her mind is sharp even if her body is frail. It's easy to see where Paul gets his easygoing nature from.

We take a walk around the meadow at the back of the trailer park, and Donna insists we stay for lunch. She makes up boloney and cheese sandwiches, and we eat them at the outdoor table while watching the kids play.

When we leave, she hugs me with a tight grip, and I promise to come back and visit soon.

We get back to Paul's place and go inside. It's quiet compared to the rowdy trailer park and I think about how different our worlds are, how different our upbringings have been.

"What's up?" Paul asks.

I lean my elbows on the kitchen counter. "You must think I'm a privileged princess."

He shakes his head. "No, Cassie. I think you're fucking amazing."

He takes my hands in his, and his expression is sincere. It doesn't matter to Paul that we're different, and it shouldn't matter to me.

I may have had a privileged upbringing, but no one encouraged me to follow my dreams the way Paul does. No one gives me that kind of confidence.

He pulls me onto his lap and his hands move down my cheeks, brushing my hair behind my ears.

"You're fucking amazing, Cassie. And I love you."

The words make my heart sing. This has happened so quickly, and I'm speechless as emotions bubble up inside me.

I'm about to answer him back when the sound of a car pulling up outside makes us both turn toward the window.

A familiar gray Audi pulls into the clearing.

It's my dad.

11

CASSIE

*D*ad's expression is thunderous as he storms toward the front door. I pull it open before he can reach it and step out onto the porch, with Paul right behind me. Paul puts his hand on my shoulder and squeezes, and his support gives me the confidence I need to face my dad.

"If you came here to intimidate me, it's not going to work."

His gaze shifts from me to Paul, and the hand that's resting on my shoulder. His frown deepens.

"Okay, Cassie," Dad says. "You've got our attention. Your mom is going to cancel her work trip next week, and we'll spend some time with you. You can come home now."

He still thinks this is just about me wanting attention. Maybe that's how it started, but it's more than that now. I've learned who I can be. Paul has taught me that. He taught me that being myself is okay, and the things I want from life are okay. I'll never be that person living under my parents' roof.

I stick my chin out and fold my arms across my chest. "No."

Dad falters, and confusion passes over his face. "What do you mean no?"

"I mean, I'm not coming home. I choose to stay here." I turn to Paul, hoping that this is okay. "If you'll have me."

Paul's eyes light up. "Of course. You don't need to ask."

He cups my chin with his hand and presses a gentle kiss to my lips.

My dad splutters. "I said you don't have to pretend anymore, Cassie. You've got our attention."

I turn back to my father. "I'm not pretending, Dad. I love Paul."

I hold Paul's hand and stand tall. I want Dad to see the truth of it. I want him to see *me* for who I am. I'm not just his daughter he can parade around at their functions. I'm a person in my own right. I have hopes and dreams and feelings. I have a heart, and my heart loves Paul.

Paul takes a step forward. "I love your daughter. I'll treat her right, like she deserves. I'll take care of her and protect her, and it's not just me. Cassie now has an entire family to look out for her at the club."

My dad's brows shoot up. "The club?"

"Yes," Paul says. "The one with the award-winning brewery. And the restaurant that tourists flock to dine at. *That* club."

Dad harrumphs and looks away. He knows a good

business when he sees it. I'm sure he's dug into the MC's business ventures, and there's no denying the club has good business sense.

"Is that really what you want?" Dad gestures to the tiny cabin and the simple plant holders full of herbs. "I'm sure you're a nice guy, Paul, but you can't give Cassie what she needs. This place… it's not good enough for my Cassie."

Anger flares inside me. "You don't know what I need, Dad. You think a big house and fine clothes is all that I need? But I'm happier here with a cozy armchair and a bookcase full of books. I don't need much, but what I do need is love. Paul loves me. He sees me for who I *am*. That's what I need."

Paul steps forward and squeezes my hand. "I can give Cassie exactly what she needs. Love, support and my unwavering loyalty."

He looks at me as he says it, and my chest warms. A grin breaks out on my face, and no matter what my father says, I've found my new home.

"This place is too small," Dad mutters, stuck on the practicalities. "What is it, one bedroom?"

"But it's got two bookcases," I say.

Paul grins at me. "I know a bunch of guys who are pretty handy with woodwork. We'll expand the cabin as our family grows."

Dad's eyes almost bug out of his head. And that makes me giggle.

"You want kids?"

Paul smiles sheepishly. "Of course, if that's what you want."

My chest explodes with happiness. I have a vision of our kids running around the cabin while I write in the evenings. I squeeze Paul's hand.

My dad's eyes dart toward our hands, and something changes in him. He rakes a hand through his hair, and he lets out a long sigh. He doesn't like it, but he knows when he's beat.

"Your mother won't be happy."

"Mom will get used to it," I say.

"You'd better both come out for dinner next week, Cassie. I want to get to know the man who's in love with my daughter."

"Even better," Paul says. "Why don't you and your wife come here? I'll cook for you."

My dad's eyes widen. "You cook?"

"Everything from scratch." He tugs at his beard. "I'll have to get a couple more chairs, but we can manage."

My dad harrumphs. "I'll speak to your mother."

I suddenly have a wave of affection for my father. He's been too caught up in his business to spend much time with me, but he does love me. I race down the steps and plant a kiss on his cheek.

"Thank you, Dad."

"I just want you to be happy, Cassie. I want you to have everything you deserve in life."

"Don't worry," I say. "I will."

We watch him drive off, taking the gravel road slow so as not to get chips in the paintwork of the Audi.

"Did you mean what you said?" Paul asks.

"Every word of it." I turn to face him, and his breath is warm on my cheek. "I'm yours, Paul."

The heat of his breath warms my entire body. I tilt my neck, giving him access to my throat.

"Good." His lips tickle my neck. "Now it's time to claim you."

12
PAUL

I take Cassie's hand in mine and lead her into the cabin and straight to the bedroom. She turns to face me, and I draw her close.

"I meant what I said, Cassie. Stay here, stay with me. I don't have much, but everything I have is yours."

"I meant it too," she said. "Everything I need is right here in this room."

I cup her cheeks in my palms. I've waited so long for this woman. I've seen her blossom from a shy teenager into a young woman who knows who she is. And she's everything I need in my life.

Her hair has fallen over her face, and I sweep it back, letting my fingers trail down to her throat.

My hand moves to the back of her head and tangles in her hair. I pull her close as my lips kiss her smooth cheek.

I love you, Cassie." My mouth moves down the line of her jaw.

"I love you too, Paul."

Our lips meet, and her soft lips on mine makes me instantly hard. I've waited a long time to claim Cassie.

Her hands slide under my jacket, and she slides it off my shoulders. It drops to the floor with a thud. Our bodies collide, and the kiss turns hungry. I draw her to me as my hands slide around her waist, pulling her closer. Her hips grind against mine, and a groan erupts from my throat.

"I've waited a long time for this," she moans.

"So have I. You'll never be alone again, Cassie. Move in with me. I don't have much to offer, but everything I have is yours. My heart, my soul, my love and protection. I'll worship your body and love you every day for as long as I live."

I cup her cheeks in my hands, and her eyes are wet.

"I hope those are happy tears."

"They are. You're the first person to really see me."

I chuckle, because she has no idea how long I've watched her. "I first saw you five years ago, when you were an awkward eighteen-year-old sneaking into the White Heart with Isabella and fake IDs."

She chuckles at the memory. "Until Isabella's body-guards came for us."

I look into her eyes, because I want her to understand what I'm saying.

"I noticed you then, Cassie. The instant I saw you tugging at that too-tight skirt and tottering on heels you weren't used to wearing, with the top of a book poking out of your purse. I knew you'd be mine someday."

SADIE KING

"Then why did it take you five years?"

"I had to wait for you to grow up. I had to give you a chance to experience life, Cassie. But I never stopped loving you."

She melts against me, and I pull her into my chest. My arm snakes down her back and over her hips. "And I'll never stop loving you."

I kiss her hard, and our tongues collide. I can't get enough of her sweetness, and I pull her hard against me. But I need more.

I walk us backward until her knees touch the bed. "Are you ready to be my woman?"

"Yes," she whispers. "I'm ready."

I push her back onto the bed and run my fingers down her torso. My hand comes to the top of her leggings and I tug them down slowly, the tips of my fingers trailing down her thighs. I pull them over her ankles and discard them on the floor.

I take her leg in my hand and kiss her ankle. Cassie trembles.

"Are you cold?"

"No," she says, sitting up on her elbows. "It tickles."

"Tickles good or tickles bad?" I say, as I graze my beard over her ankle.

"Tickles good." She squirms.

I plant little kisses up her calf until I get to her knee. "How about here?" I lift her leg so my beard trails roughly over the back of her knee.

She whimpers. "That tickles, but in a good way, if you know what I mean."

Oh, I know what she means.

I continue moving up her leg, kissing her inner thigh, letting my beard scrape against her soft skin as I get closer to the apex of her thighs. When I reach the top, my mouth moves over her panties. The fabric is damp with her arousal, the musky scent heady and intoxicating. I let out a warm breath through the fabric.

Cassie whimpers. "That feels good."

"It's my job to make you feel good, Cassie."

I hook my hands over her panties and pull them down her thighs, taking them off quicker than I did her leggings.

My hands slide up her legs, and I clutch her inner thighs. I spread her legs apart and bury my face between them.

Cassie gasps as I kiss her, and her sweet nectar cascades onto my tongue.

One hand slides up under her top until I find her breast. I pull the bra back and tug at her nipple, gently at first, then harder to match the movement of my tongue.

Cassie writhes under me. Her legs lock around my shoulders, and her moans get louder until she's crying out my name. I'll never tire of those sweet little sounds.

Her pussy pulses with release, and my tongue is soaked in her juices. I wait for her pussy to stop throbbing before I sit back on my knees.

Cassie is lying back on the bed, primed and ready.

"Are you ready for me?"

She lifts her head and pants, "I'm ready, Paul. I want you to take my virginity. It's all yours. I'm all yours."

Her words pierce me deep in my soul. She's giving herself to me, and I don't take that lightly. I vow silently to look after this woman every day of my life. I'll make her mine officially as soon as I can with a quick wedding, although her parents will probably want something bigger.

I stand up and pull my T-shirt off, then discard my pants. Cassie removes her top and slides back on the bed to make room for me. We lie next to each other, naked together completely for the first time.

My hand runs from her shoulder, down her torso and over her hip. Her curves are soft under my touch.

"You're beautiful, Cassie."

I press my lips to her breast as my hips push forward, needing to feel my dick pressed against her. Her thighs open, and I slide between the gap. Her pussy lips suck onto me, and I almost lose it right there.

"Fuck, Cassie. I won't last long."

"That's okay. I want to make you feel good too, Paul."

"You already do, baby."

My hips move back and forth in slow, torturous movements. My lips close on her nipple, and she tilts her head back and sucks in a breath.

My hands cup her buttocks, and I moan at the softness of her flesh under my rough hands.

"I don't want to use a condom." I pull back so I can see her expression. "I want to get you pregnant. I want to tie you to me, Cassie."

Her eyes go wide. "You want to start a family?"

"With you, I do." I want nothing more than to have

Cassie's little babies running around our cabin. I want to read books to them by the fire, and they can help me feed the chickens.

"I want that too." Her voice is barely a whisper.

I roll her onto her back; I want to see her staring straight at me as I enter her.

I part her thighs and run my hands over her pussy. She's dripping wet and I ease my fingers in, making sure she's primed for me. Cassie bucks her hips, and I rub my palm in little circles on her clit as she arches her back.

"If you keep doing that, I'm going to come before you get inside me."

"That's good, baby. You do that."

I take her nipple in my mouth and tug on it softly. Her moans increase with every movement.

She grips the sheets, and her pussy convulses around my fingers. Her clit throbs, and watching her come undone almost makes me lose it.

I pull my finger out and slide the tip of my dick inside her.

She gasps and sits up on her elbows. "I don't think it's going to fit," she says, a tremor in her voice.

I kiss her gently. "Relax, baby. It might hurt for a little, but I promise you, I'll fit. You were made for me, Cassie. Trust me."

I take her leg and push her thighs wide open, dragging one leg over my shoulder. I push in further, and she squeezes her eyes shut.

"Eyes on me, Cassie." It comes out as a groan, because I don't know how much longer I can hold it together.

Her pussy squeezes my dick, and it's like nothing I've ever experienced before.

Our eyes lock and our breathing synchronizes. "You ready, baby?"

She nods, and I push all the way inside her.

The sensation is overwhelming, and I cry out at the same moment she does. My grip tightens on her thigh, and I hold on to her. Our eyes lock and hers are wide, in awe or pain, I'm not sure.

"I love you, Cassie." I want to make it known in this moment.

"Oh, yes," she breathes.

I feel her begin to relax. I pull out a little and thrust in again. She cries out, and her pussy squeezes so tight I have to hold on to the bed sheets.

"Fuck. Not going to last."

"Neither am I."

She's panting hard, and so am I. I grab her other leg and throw it over my shoulder. This time, I thrust deep. I want to bury myself deep inside of Cassie. She cries out, and her hips slam upward to meet mine.

I drive in and out of her, thrusting harder and harder as her whimpers grow louder and louder.

My balls pull up tight as she pants my name.

"Come for me, baby."

Cassie screams my name as the orgasm shatters through her body. As she releases, I let myself go.

"Cassie!" I bellow as I erupt inside her, my cum exploding out of me to coat her womb.

We stay like this for a long time as waves of pleasure

wrap around us. Only when my cock stops throbbing, do I slide out of her.

We lie facing each other on the bed and I pull her close, kissing her face.

"Are you okay?"

"More than okay." She peers up at me shyly. "I feel like myself for the first time."

I kiss her gently as my heart expands.

"That's what I want, my sweet, shy bookworm. You can always be yourself here, Cassie. I love you exactly as you are."

She sighs contentedly and settles into my arms. We stay right there, holding each other tight until we fall asleep.

EPILOGUE

CASSIE

Three weeks later...

*T*he aroma of smoking meat fills the air outside the clubhouse as Arlo lifts the lid off the smoker to check on the ribs.

He peels a piece of meat off and stuffs it in his mouth, chewing loudly as he makes appreciative noises.

"Meat's ready."

I look up from my book and shift against Paul. We're sitting at one of the picnic tables outside the clubhouse a little away from the group. I've got my feet up on the bench, leaning against him while we both read.

"I'll go help bring the salads out."

His arm slides around my waist, and he pulls me against him as he nuzzles into my neck. "If you go, I'll be left reading on my own. And that's just anti-social."

I wiggle around to face him, and he plants a soft kiss on my lips. "I hate to break it to you, but it's considered rude to read through dinner with your friends."

He chuckles and kisses me again. "Remind me why we're here again?"

He's only half joking. At home, in Paul's cabin, we've initiated the reading dinner. Not every night, but if one of us is in the middle of an unput-downable book, or if we just don't feel like talking, we'll both read our books while we eat.

To outsiders it might appear strange, like we don't have anything to talk about. But for us, it means we're comfortable enough with each other that we don't need to talk. I love our reading dinners, and our nights sitting side by side in armchairs with the fire going and a good book each.

Some nights, instead of reading, I write.

I finished my first book, and Paul helped me figure out how to self-publish. I put my book up for sale and was surprised that some people bought it, and they left good reviews. I've since written another and am onto my third.

I love writing short over the top alien romance, and there are readers who love my stories. It's not bringing in much money, but I don't need much. I'm happy, and I feel like myself for the first time in years. That's all I need.

I extract myself from Paul and head into the club-house kitchen.

"The meat's ready," I let Isabella know.

She claps her hands together and stands up from the

chair that's been dragged in for her. "Right ladies." She takes charge; as the old lady of the Prez, the women listen to her. Isabella expertly directs who to take out salads and who to take out plates and cutlery. She gives tasks to some of the older children who are keen to help.

I grab a bowl of pasta salad from the fridge and carry it outside.

Soon we're all seated on the picnic tables passing plates of food around. There's the sound of easy chatter and the clinking of cutlery. The kids are at a small table of their own with Isla and Luke sitting with them, helping whoever needs it.

Paul is on one side of me and Sydney on the other. "Do you want some soda, Cassie?" Sydney asks.

She pours me a glass full and tops up her own. "How are the books going?" she asks.

I swallow my mouthful. "Good."

She raises an eyebrow. "Just good? Specs was telling me you've sold a bunch of copies and you're onto your third book."

Heat creeps up my neck, and I steal a glance at Paul. I hate talking about myself, but he gives me an encouraging smile.

I turn back to Sydney and search her expression for any sign she's teasing me. But she seems genuinely interested.

After so long in fear of being judged, it's hard to talk to people about my writing.

Isabella's cackle from the next table has me glancing up. She's got a forkful of food in one hand and the other arm is around Raiden. I missed the joke, but she catches my eye and gives me a big grin.

I glance around at the tables of bikers and their women and the gaggle of children. They're my family now, and there is no judgement here.

I turn back to Sydney. "Better than good, actually. It's going really well." I tell her about the books I've sold and the next plot I'm working on. She listens intently, genuinely interested.

The clinking of glass has everyone falling silent. Raiden stands up and clears his throat.

"It's great to see everyone here tonight, and there's something special we're celebrating."

Paul slides his arm around my waist, and I lean against him.

"We have a talented bunch of people in this club," Raiden continues. "And now we have our first published author."

Heads turn to our table, and heat spreads up my neck.

"Congratulations, Cassie, on your first published book."

I'm not used to attention, and I want to burrow into Paul. But when I look around at the expectant faces with their glasses raised in a toast, a different kind of warmth spreads though me.

I found a place where I belong, where I'm accepted for who I am. A place where I'm seen.

"Thank you." Tears spring to my eyes as I raise my glass to my big biker family.

Paul nuzzles my neck, and Sydney gives my hand a friendly squeeze.

I'm saved from giving a speech by the roar of a motorcycle.

All heads turn as a Harley pulls into the compound.

Paul tenses next to me, and Raiden extracts himself from the picnic table along with some of the other men.

Everyone from the club is here today, and by the tense expressions on the faces of the men, we're not expecting company.

The Harley pulls to a stop, and a large man clad in biking leathers slides off it. He's broad-shouldered and tall, well over six foot. He slides off his helmet to reveal shaggy blonde hair and a wild beard.

The man's weather-lined face is serious as he scans the bikers.

His crystal blue eyes find Sydney's, and he smiles. "Hello cupcake."

Sydney gasps.

I turn to face her, and she's gone pale.

"Who's that?" I ask, but she's too focused on the man to hear me.

"Viking!" roars Raiden. "When the fuck did you get back?"

The man called Viking strolls over to the group, and Raiden throws his arms around him in greeting.

Sydney stands abruptly, making the table wobble. She has to place a hand on her tight black leather skirt to extract herself from the picnic table, and her tattooed hands tremble as she picks up her soda. With her thick eyeliner, knee-length boots, and dark hair, cupcake is not the nickname I'd associate with Sydney.

While the men greet the new arrival, Sydney approaches him with her drink in hand. Her brother Nate pushes out from his place at the table and walks quickly to stand behind her. He's the only man here not happy to see the new arrival.

Viking is released from a man hug from Barrels, and he turns to Sydney. Even from here, I see the softness in his expression when it lands on her.

"I heard you were back," he says.

Silence fills the courtyard as all eyes are on them. They stare at each other, Viking's eyes soft, while Sydney's burn with rage. Then she launches her drink at him. He gasps as she spins around and heads into the clubhouse with Nate following close behind.

The man looks after her in dismay as soda drips off his beard. Whoever this Viking guy is, not everyone is pleased to see him back.

* * *

BONUS CONTENT

Not ready to say goodbye to Paul and Carrie? Get a glimpse into their life when this book-loving couple have kids. Read the Wild Desire bonus scene when you sign up to the Sadie King newsletter.

Read the bonus scene at:
authorsadieking.com/bonus-scenes

Already a subscriber? Check your last email for the link that will take you straight to all the bonus content and free books.

BOOKS & SERIES BY SADIE KING

Wild Heart Mountain

Jake's Heroes

These ex-Navy SEALs will do anything for the women they fall for. Expect wounded warriors in these emotional and steamy stories of love and healing.

Military Heroes

Kobe brings together a group of military veterans who live on the side of Wild Heart Mountain. Can these wounded warriors find love or do their scars cut too deep?

Wild Riders MC

This group of ex-military bikers fall hard and fall fast when they encounter the curvy women who heal their hearts.

Knocked Up

A side story to the Wild Rider's MC. A secret baby romance featuring an ex-military demolition man who thinks he's not worthy of love.

Mountain Heroes

Steamy stories featuring the men and women from Wild Heart Mountain's Search and Rescue and Fire service.

Biker Brothers of Winter Town

Short, sweet tales of men who ride and the curvy women who claim their hearts.

Temptation

A damaged hero and a lost virgin in an explosive instalove retelling of the Hansel and Gretel story set in the woods of Wild Heart Mountain.

A Runaway Bride for Christmas

A snowstorm keeps this runaway bride trapped in the cabin of the mountain's biggest grump.

A Secret Baby for Christmas

Mr. Porter's Christmas takes a surprise turn when his daughter's best friend turns up with his baby.

Sunset Coast

Underground Crows MC

Short and steamy MC romance stories of obsessed men and curvy girls.

Sunset Security

A security firm run by ex-military men who become obsessed with their curvy girls.

His Christmas Obsession

A Christmas romance about an obsessed biker who rides across the country in the snow to reach Cleo before he's even met her.

Men of the Sea

Super short and steamy tales from Temptation Bay of bad boys and curvy girls.

Love and Obsession

A bad boy trilogy featuring a thief, a henchman and an ex-military hitman who finds redemption with his curvy girl.

Filthy Rich Love

The billionaires of the Sunset Coast. These alpha men fall hard and fall fast for the younger curvy women who crash into their world.

His Big Book Stack

The Underground Crows are called in to help an old friend do some digging when the woman he's obsessed with is threatened.

Maple Springs

Small Town Sisters

Five curvy sister's inherit a dog hotel. But can they find love? Short and steamy instalove romance!

Candy's Café

A small-town cafe that's all heart. Meet the sister's who run it and the customer's who keep coming back.

All the Single Dads

These single dad hotties are fiercely protective and will do anything for the ones they love.

Men of Maple Mountain

These men are OTT possessive and will stop at nothing to claim the curvy innocent women they become obsessed with.

All the Scars we Cannot See

An instalove mountain man romance featuring a scarred ex-military recluse and a curvy girl on the run who steals his heart.

The Carter Family

Blue collar men find love with curvy girls in these quick read instalove romances.

Curvy Girls Can

Short, sweet and steamy instalove stories about sassy curvy women and the men who love them.

The Biker Brother's Curvy Christmas

Hot Santas, curvy girls and bikers. A feel good Christmas romance duet.

What the Fudge

A grumpy/sunshine Christmas romance.

Fudge and the Firefighter

A hot firefighter and curvy girl instalove Christmas romance.

The Seal's Obsession

A soft stalker, secret baby, military romance. Featuring an OTT obsessed alpha male and a sassy curvy girl.

Kings County

Kings of Fire

Smoking hot tales of insta-love, featuring brave heroes and sassy heroines that will melt your heart.

King's Cops

Do you love police romance books? Then the King's Cops series is for you! Short, sweet and steamy tales of insta-love, featuring brave heroes and sassy heroines that will melt your heart.

For a full list of Sadie King's books check out her website

www.authorsadieking.com

ABOUT THE AUTHOR

Sadie King is a USA Today Best Selling Author of contemporary romance novellas.

She lives in New Zealand with her ex-military husband and raucous young son.

When she's not writing she loves catching waves with her son, running along the beach, and drinking good wine with a book in hand.

Keep in touch when you sign up for her newsletter. You'll snag yourself a free short romance and access to all the bonus content!

authorsadieking.com/bonus-scenes

Printed in Dunstable, United Kingdom